GOOD TO BE GREEN

Rubbish or Recyling?

Written by DEBORAH CHANCELLOR
Illustrated by DIANE EWEN

A story about rubbish and why ....ant to recycle

WAYLAND

It was a rainy
weekend.
Nasir and Nadia
were bored.

But then Nadia had
a brainwave.
"Let's make a junk
model!" she said.

3

"Shall we make a robot?" asked Nasir.

"Great idea!" said Nadia.

"We can enter it for the school competition."

"We need to use things that can be **recycled**," said Nadia. She picked a can out of the kitchen bin.

"We can call our model a recycling robot."

Cans made of a metal called **aluminium** can be recycled to make new cans, or used to make parts for planes and bikes.

Nasir and Nadia made a pile of things that can be recycled, and a pile of things that can't.

We need to sort out our **rubbish**! Over half of the rubbish that ends up in our dustbins could be recycled instead. We can recycle paper, cardboard, glass, most metals and some kinds of plastic.

"Look at all this **plastic**!" said Nasir.

"It's a shame we can't recycle it," said Nadia.

Dad came into
the kitchen.
"What a mess!" he said.

"We need to go to the **rubbish dump**," said Dad.

The twins helped carry all the plastic to the car.

Plastic rubbish can be harmful to **wildlife**.
Sadly, lots of it ends up in the sea. We all need
to use less plastic to stop this happening.

The twins were shocked by what they saw at the rubbish dump.

Garden Waste

Paper and Cardboard

"Look at all this **waste**!" said Nasir.

"Can any of it be recycled?" asked Nadia.

"Some of it can," said Dad.

"What about the rest?" asked Nasir.

"It will be buried at a **landfill site**," said Dad.

When plastic is thrown out, it takes a long time to break down into safe, natural materials. Some plastic bottles take five hundred years to do this.

The twins didn't like
this idea very much.

"We must recycle as
much as we can,"
said Nadia.

"And re-use what
we can't recycle,"
said Nasir.

We need to **re-use** things instead of throwing them away. Don't throw out your old toys – share them with someone else instead!

Back at home, Nasir and Nadia
began building their junk model.

The twins worked very hard
and the day flew by in a flash.

"Look at our Recycling Robot!" said Nadia.

"Wow!" said Dad. "It's amazing!"

Re-use things made from glass, metal and plastic.
It saves the energy needed to recycle them
or make replacements.

The twins couldn't wait to take their junk model to school. They entered the competition and won first prize!

The Recycling Robot helped everyone
sort out recycling from rubbish.

Quiz time

Which of these things are true?

Read the book again to find out!

(Cover up the answers on page 27.)

1. It is impossible to recycle a can of drink.

2. Over half of the rubbish we throw out could be recycled instead.

3. Plastic rubbish often ends up in the sea.

4. Plastic bottles can take up to five years to break down into safe materials.

5. We can't reuse things that are made of glass.

Answers

1. **False:**  Aluminium cans are recycled to make parts for planes and bikes. *(See page 7)*

2. **True:**  We need to sort our rubbish more carefully. *(See page 9)*

3. **True:**  Lots of plastic waste ends up in the sea and is harmful to sea life. *(See page 13)*

4. **False:**  Plastic bottles can take up to five hundred years to do this. *(See page 17)*

5. **False:**  Glass can be re-used. This saves the energy it takes to make new glass. *(See page 23)*

Get active

In the story, Nasir and Nadia use recycled rubbish to make a junk model of a robot. Think of some other models you could make with recycled rubbish, such as a space ship or a time machine. Then collect and sort some rubbish for recycling, to make a model of your own.

Collect some materials that can be recycled, and some that can't. Use scraps of these materials to make a collage all about recycling.

Try to find out about sea animals and birds that are in danger because of plastic pollution, for example the green turtle and the albatross. Ask an adult to help you find out more. You could watch a TV documentary, read a book or look at an environment website together.

Make a short film about plastic pollution in the oceans. You could use the video camera on a smartphone to do this. Think carefully about what you want to say before you begin and make a simple storyboard (a series of drawings showing each scene) before you start filming. You could include photos of endangered sea creatures and plastic rubbish that has been washed up on beaches.

Glossary

aluminium   a metal that can be recycled (made into something new)

energy   power that is used to make something work, for example electricity

landfill site   a place where rubbish is buried in the ground

plastic   a machine-made material that can be moulded into any shape

recycled   when rubbish is changed into something useful

re-use   to use something again

rubbish   things you throw away because you don't need them anymore

rubbish dump   a place where you take things you don't want anymore

waste   things that are not wanted, or can't be used again

wildlife   animals that are not tame and live in their natural habitat

A note about sharing this book

The GOOD TO BE GREEN series provides a starting point for further discussion on important environmental issues, such as pollution, climate change and endangered wildlife. The topics considered in each book are relevant to all, children and adults alike.

Rubbish or Recycling?

This story explores, in a familiar context, some issues surrounding recycling. **Rubbish or Recycling?** demonstrates key concepts on this theme, such as the need to sort our household waste carefully, so that as much of it is recycled as possible. It also covers the concept of re-using everyday items, to save the energy it takes to manufacture replacements. The story and the non-fiction elements in **Rubbish or Recycling?** encourage the reader to conclude that we all need to recycle more of our rubbish, as doing so is good for the environment and helps to save endangered wildlife.

How to use the book

The story is designed for adults to share with either an individual child or a group of children, and as a starting point for discussion. The book provides visual support to build confidence in children who are starting to read on their own.

The story introduces vocabulary that is relevant to the theme of recycling, such as: *'waste'*, *'rubbish'*, *'recycling'*, *'re-use'*, *'landfill site'*, *'glass'*, *'metal'*, *'plastic'*, *'aluminium'*.

Some of the vocabulary in the story and information panels will be unfamiliar to the reader. These words are in bold text, and they are defined in the Glossary at the back of the book (see page 29). When reading the story for the first time, refer to the Glossary with the children, to check they understand what the words in bold mean.

There is also an Index at the back of the book, a standard feature of non-fiction books. Encourage the children to use the index when you are talking about the book - for example, ask them to use the index to find the page that shows a landfill site (page 16). This useful research skill can be practised at a very early age. It is important that children know that information can be found in books as well as searched for on the internet.

Before reading the story

Pick a time to read when you and the children are relaxed and can take time to share the story together. Before you start reading, look at the illustrations and discuss what the book may be about.

After reading, talk about the book with the children

Discuss the story together, perhaps asking the following questions:
- What do Nasir and Nadia use to make their robot? *(see pages 6-7)*
- How do Nasir and Nadia sort out their rubbish? *(see pages 8-9)*
- Why do they go to the rubbish dump? *(see pages 10-12)*
- What kind of rubbish do they take with them? *(see pages 12-13)*
- What do they learn about recycling? *(see pages 16-17, pages 18-19)*

Look at the information panels, then talk together about recycling.
You could ask the following questions:
- What kind of materials can be recycled? *(see pages 6-7, pages 8-9)*
- What happens to rubbish that is not recycled? *(see page 16)*
- Why is plastic bad for the planet? *(see page 13)*
- How can we reduce the amount of plastic we use? *(see pages 18-19)*
- What kind of things can we re-use?
  (see page 23)
- Why is it good to re-use things?
  (see page 23)

Do the Quiz together *(see pages 26-27)*.
It may help to re-read the information
panels if the children's answers are wrong,
or they just seem to be guessing!

Index

First published in Great Britain in 2019
by Wayland
Copyright © Hodder and Stoughton, 2019

All rights reserved

Editor: Sarah Peutrill
Designer: Cathryn Gilbert

ISBN (HB): 978 1 5263 0886 3
ISBN (PB): 978 1 5263 0887 0

Printed in China

Wayland, an imprint of
Hachette Children's Group
Part of Hodder and Stoughton
Carmelite House
50 Victoria Embankment
London EC4Y 0DZ

An Hachette UK Company
www.hachette.co.uk
www.hachettechildrens.co.uk

MIX
Paper from
responsible sources
FSC® C104740
FSC
www.fsc.org